This book belongs to

. . . .

A DORLING KINDERSLEY BOOK

First American Edition, 1994

2 4 6 8 10 9 7 5 3 1

Published in the United States by
Dorling Kindersley Publishing Inc., 95 Madison Avenue,
New York, New York 10016

Library of Congress Cataloging-in-Publication Data
Winter, Susan
A Baby just like me / by Susan Winter. —1st American ed.
p.   cm.
Summary: Although at first she is disappointed with her new baby
sister, Martha comes to appreciate her with time.
ISBN 1-56458-668-5
[1. Babies—Fiction. 2. Sisters—Fiction.] I. Title.
PZ7.W7625Mar 1994
[E]—dc20   93-49848
                                                CIP
                                                AC

Color reproduction by DOT Gradations Ltd.
Printed in Belgium by Proost.

A BABY
JUST LIKE ME

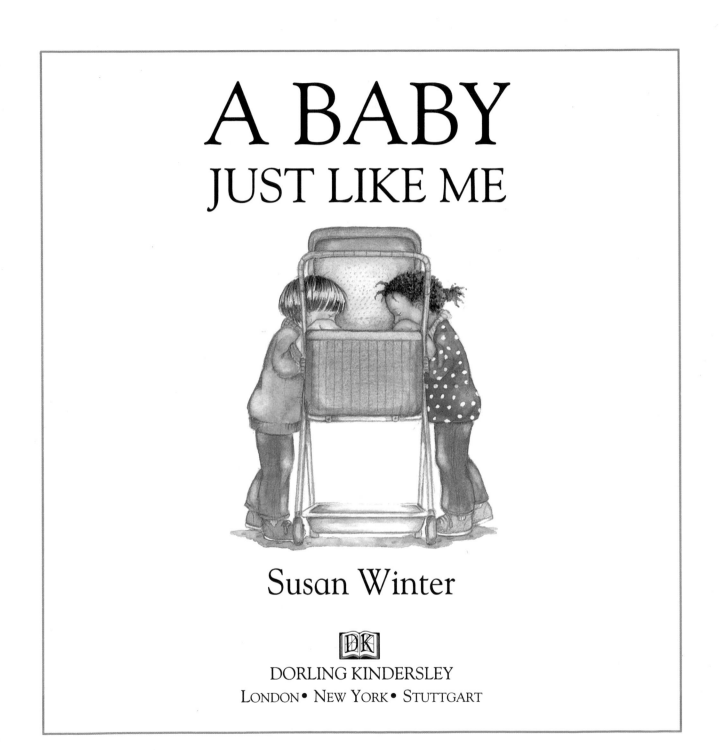

Susan Winter

DORLING KINDERSLEY
LONDON • NEW YORK • STUTTGART

Sam was spending the night at Martha's house.

They were talking about Martha's new baby sister.

"When can we see her?" asked Sam.

"Daddy says she's coming home tomorrow," said Martha.

"What's she going to do? Will she play in our band?"

"She'll do *everything*. Mommy says she's going to be just like me," Martha said proudly.

"Where's she going to sleep?" asked Sam.

"She's supposed to sleep in this basket, but I think she'll like my bottom bunk better," said Martha.

Sam and Martha got everything ready for the new baby. If she was going to be just like Martha, she could wear Martha's old baby clothes, play with her old toys, and even use her old potty.

When Martha's mommy came home,
she was carrying a bundle.

Martha and Sam peered into the bundle
and saw a tiny baby.

"She's very small," said Sam. "Are you sure
she'll be able to play with us?"
"Maybe she'll grow really quickly," Martha said.

Martha and Sam watched carefully for two whole weeks, but the baby didn't grow quickly. In fact, she didn't do much at all.

When Martha and Sam put on a puppet show for the baby, she was too busy sucking her thumb to take any notice.

When they played her their favorite tune, the baby slept right through it.

And when they made friends with a bird, the baby screamed so loudly she frightened it away!

"That baby is *not* just like you," said Sam. "She can't do anything. She's still too small to wear your clothes or play with your toys, and she can't even use a potty! Maybe you should send her back."

Martha felt funny when Sam said this.
After a while she went inside to look for
Mommy. Mommy was busy changing the
baby's diaper. Martha felt even worse.
"Can I have a cuddle?" she asked.
"Just a minute, Martha," said Mommy.

"But I need you *now*!" wailed Martha. "You're always with *her*. And she's *not* like me. She won't play with us or do anything. When is she going to be a *real* sister?"

Mommy put the baby down and scooped
Martha into her arms.

"Poor Martha," she said. "You don't remember, but you were just like that once and look how quickly you've grown."

"Did you love me as much as you love her?" asked Martha.

"Every bit as much," said Mommy, holding her tight, "and I still do."

Martha started to feel better and went back outside to play with Sam.

Mommy was right. It took a while, but finally the baby began to do more. She played in their band.

She laughed at their puppet show.

She even made friends with their bird.

"You're so lucky to have a sister," said Sam.
"I know," said Martha. "A sister just like me."